I'm a Manatee

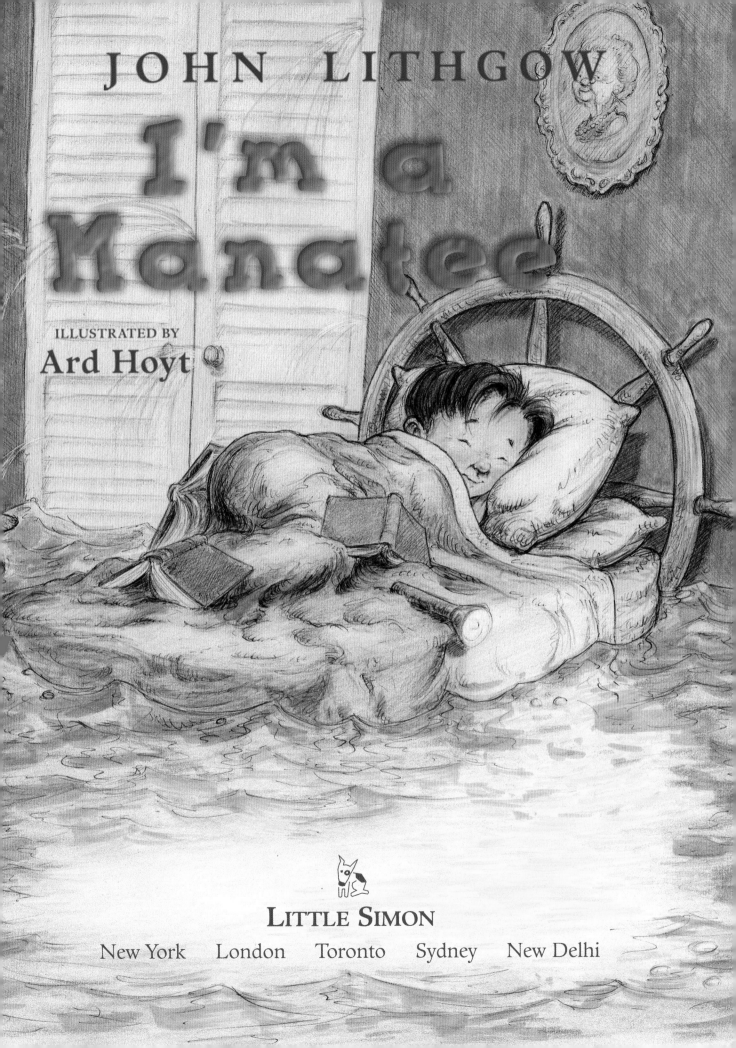

JOHN LITHGOW

I'm a Manatee

ILLUSTRATED BY
Ard Hoyt

LITTLE SIMON

New York   London   Toronto   Sydney   New Delhi

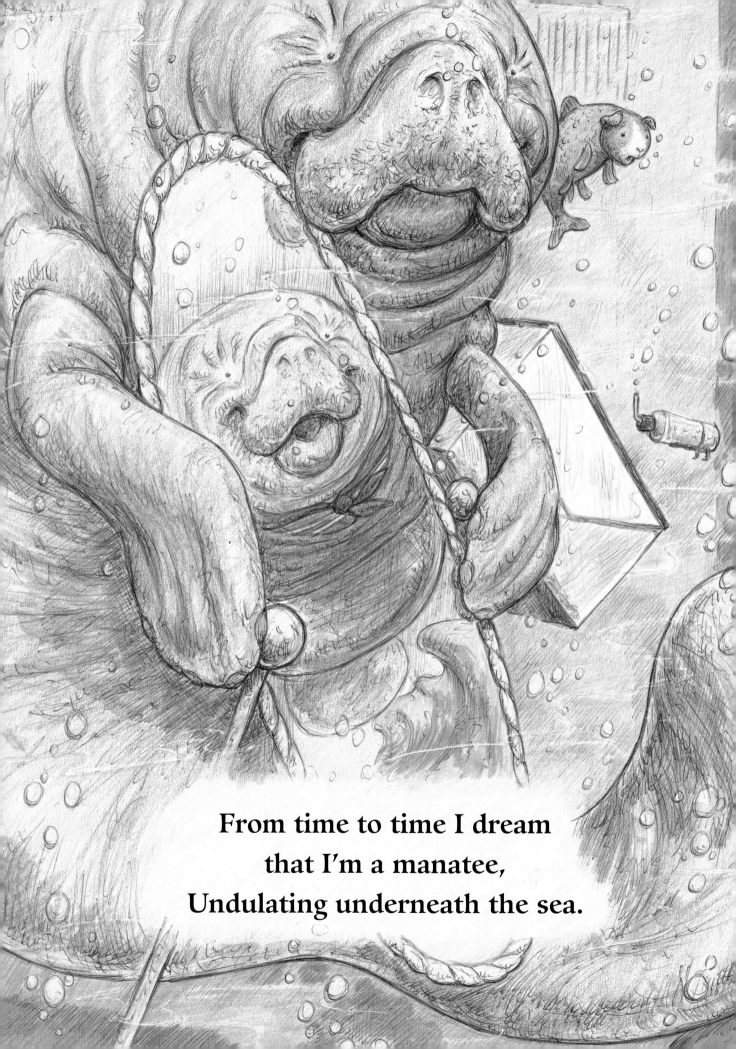

From time to time I dream
that I'm a manatee,
Undulating underneath the sea.

Unshackled by the chains of idle vanity,
A modest manatee,
That's me.

I look just like a chubby brown banana-tee
As I nose along the cozy ocean floor.
Immune from human folly and inanity,

That's why a manatee
Is such a happy herbivore.

I'm a manatee,
I'm a manatee.
I'm every bit as wrinkled as my grann-atee.

No difference between my face and fann-atee,
A noble manatee,
That's me.

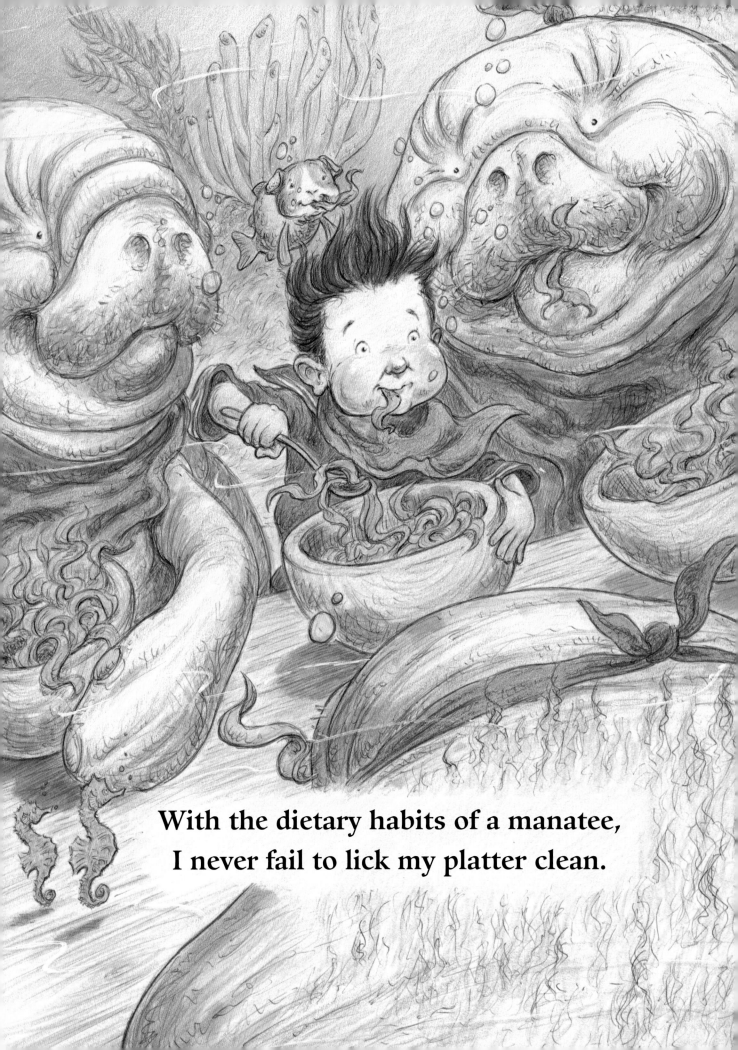

With the dietary habits of a manatee,
I never fail to lick my platter clean.

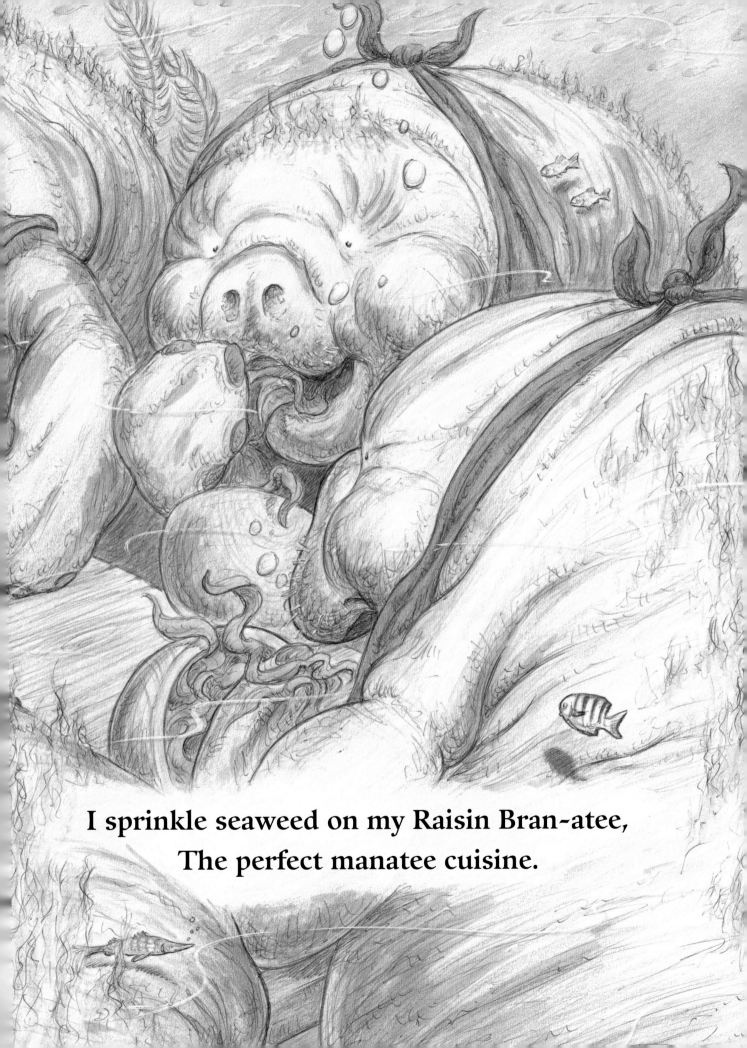

I sprinkle seaweed on my Raisin Bran-atee,
The perfect manatee cuisine.

**With my wit, sophistication, and urbanity,
I dignify my watery domain.**

No one near will ever hear me use profanity,
Because a manatee
Has his image to maintain.

I'm a manatee,
I'm a manatee.
I keep my reputation spick and span-atee.

No difference between my face and fann-atee,
A stately manatee,
That's me.

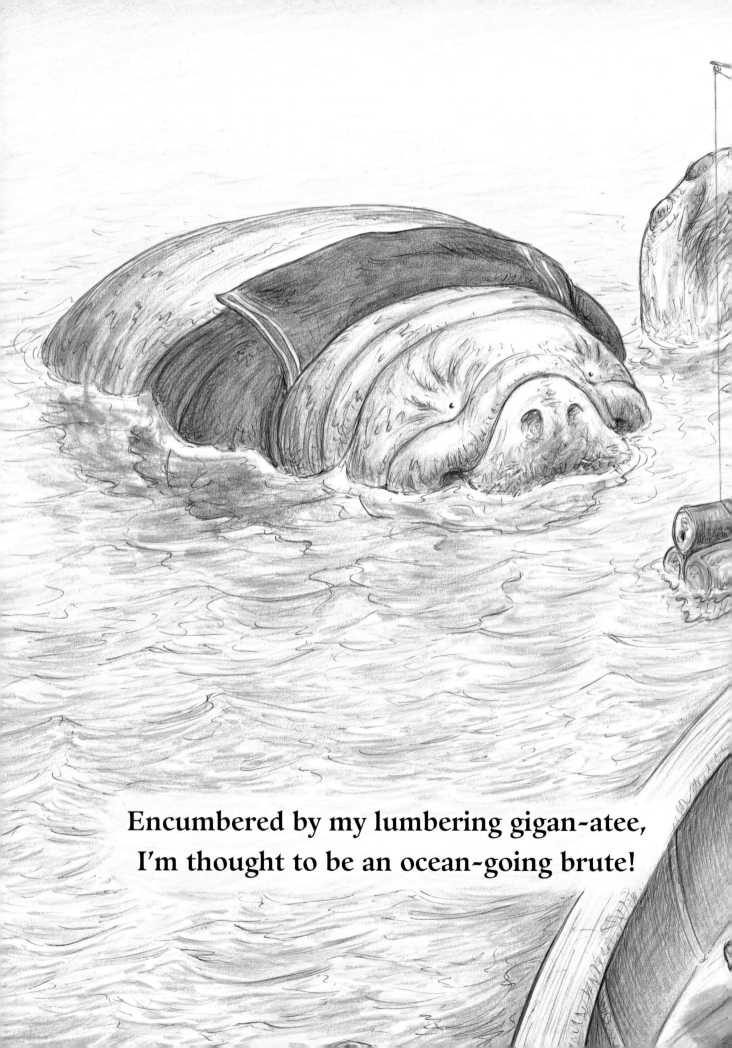

Encumbered by my lumbering gigan-atee,
I'm thought to be an ocean-going brute!

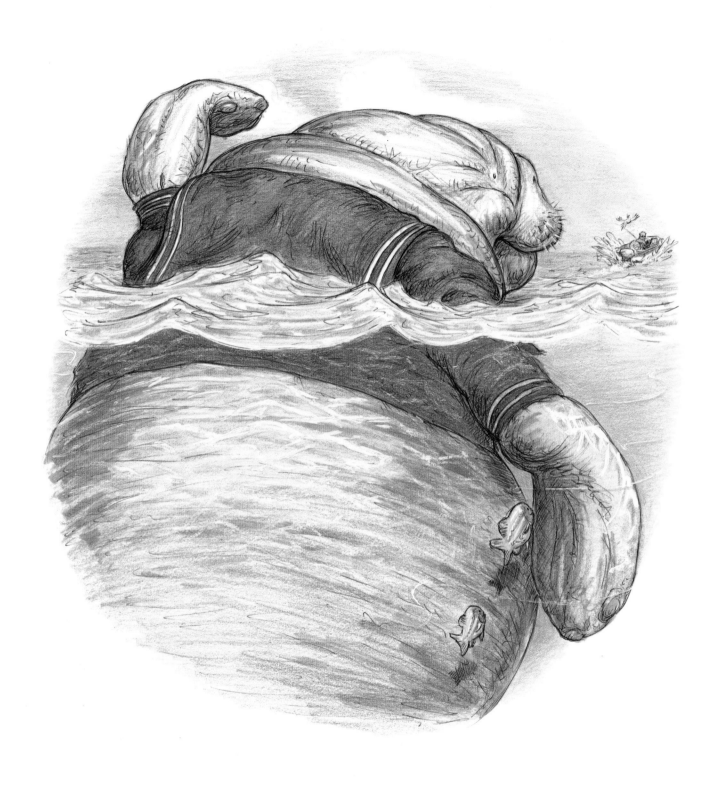

The least appealing creature on the planet-ee,

But to a manatee,
I'm cute!

I prefer my world of silence and of sanity,
But my underwater friends don't all agree.

For whenever I am dreaming I'm a manatee,
Somewhere a manatee
is dreaming that he's me!

I'm a manatee,
I'm a manatee,

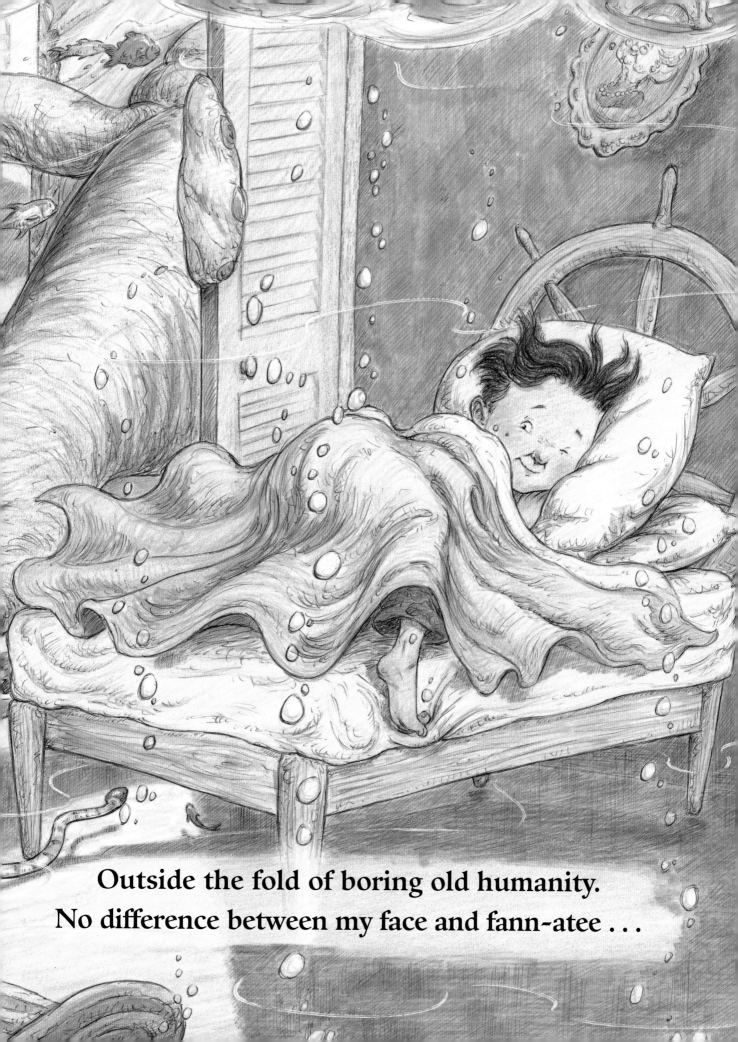

Outside the fold of boring old humanity.
No difference between my face and fann-atee . . .

I'm a roly-poly,
Jelly-rolly,
Sugar-bowly,
Heart-and-soully
Manatee . . .

That's me!

For my editor, David Gale—J. L.

To Mom and Dad—eternally glad I'm yours—A. H.

LITTLE SIMON
An imprint of Simon & Schuster Children's Publishing Division
1230 Avenue of the Americas, New York, NY 10020
Text copyright © 2003 by John Lithgow
Illustrations copyright © 2003 by Ard Hoyt
"I'm a Manatee" score copyright 2003 by Bill Elliott Music and John Lithgow
All rights for Bill Elliott Music controlled and administered by Universal Music Corp.
All rights reserved, including the right of reproduction in whole or in part in any form.
LITTLE SIMON is a registered trademark of Simon & Schuster, Inc.,
and associated colophon is a trademark of Simon & Schuster, Inc.
Also available in a Simon & Schuster Books for Young Readers hardcover edition.
Designed by Paula Winicur
Score engraving by Robert Sherwin
The text of this book was set in Guardi.
The illustrations for this book were rendered in colored pencils, pen, and ink.
For information about special discounts for bulk purchases, please contact Simon & Schuster Special Sales
at 1-866-506-1949 or business@simonandschuster.com.
The Simon & Schuster Speakers Bureau can bring authors to your live event. For more information
or to book an event contact the Simon & Schuster Speakers Bureau at
1-866-248-3049 or visit our website at www.simonspeakers.com.
Manufactured in China
This Little Simon edition 2013
10 9
The Library of Congress has cataloged the hardcover edition as follows:
Lithgow, John, 1945–
I'm a manatee / John Lithgow ; illustrated by Ard Hoyt.
p. cm.
Summary: A boy imagines that he is a manatee, sprinkling seaweed on his Raisin Bran-atee
and dignifying his watery domain with his wit, sophistication, and urbanity.
ISBN-13: 978-0-689-85427-9 (hc.)
ISBN-10: 0-689-85427-7 (hc.)
[1. Manatees—Ficiton. 2. Imagination—Fiction. 3. Stories in rhyme.]
I. Hoyt, Ard, ill. II. Title.
PZ8.3.L6375 Im 2003
[E]—dc21
2002004308
ISBN 978-0-689-85452-1 (Book and CD)
0515 SCP